G E M

Dear Hope,

This past winter was the longest, fiercest winter I remember. We were buried in drifts of snow, and that old north wind wouldn't quit. So I began thinking about spring — and especially that day you discovered a small wonder in the garden. You called him Gem. He seemed like a little miracle — it had been so long since we'd had such a visitor here. I wanted to tell the story of Gem's spring journey — all the way to my garden. This book, which took me all winter to make and which warmed the coldest days, is for you.

Love,
Gram

G E M

HOLLY HOBBIE

Little, Brown and Company
New York Boston

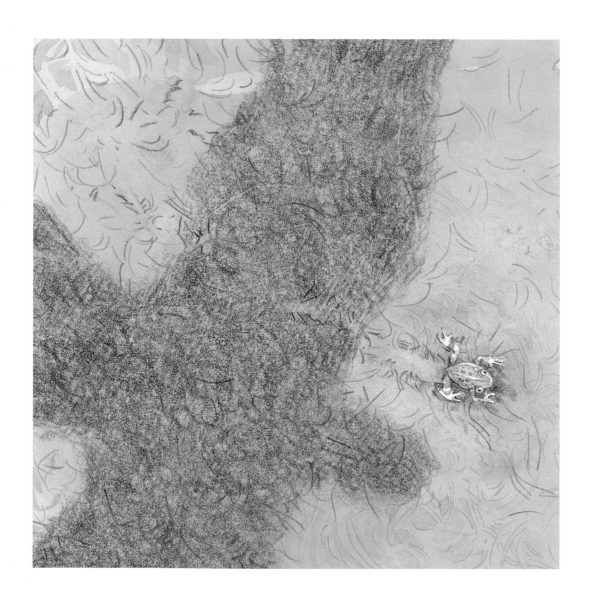

Hi Gram,

Your book about Gem just arrived, and thanks a million. It's almost like he's right in the room with me, and he is beautiful.

Some of your pictures are pretty scary, Gram. Gem is definitely a lucky old toad. I can't believe I wanted to keep him for a pet at first. Toads are not pets. They want to be free, like everything does.

My next report at school is going to be all about toads. I plan to be an expert, and I'll tell you what I find out about them. Then I want to learn about frogs. And butterflies are amazing, too. Probably everything is amazing the more you learn about it.

Thank you again for the book, which I know will keep me warm on cold, wintry days—like it did you.

And Gram, all toads are GEMS!

Your granddaughter,
Hope

Here are few more interesting things about toads:

Toads hibernate during the winter.
Some of their frog cousins have bodies that nearly freeze like Popsicles!

One toad can eat a thousand insects a day, mostly at night.
The toad snatches them out of the air with its tongue.

Toads are nocturnal—they stay up all night and sleep during the day.

Toads shed their skin. They pull it over their head like a sweater and swallow it.
The skin is good for them.

A toad can live to be forty years old—if it is very, very lucky.

When a toad is happy and healthy, that means its world is happy and healthy.
It is a very good sign.